Spike collected a jam-ja
full of frogspawn from t
pond. He held it under
Nicholas's nose.

"You've got to swallow a
spoonful," said Spike.
"Then you can be in my
gang."

But Nicholas can't do it so
he gets bashed up and
turned out of the gang's
camp. One of the pieces of
frogspawn survives,
however, and it grows and
grows and grows until it
becomes what must be the
biggest tadpole in the
world – the Killer
Tadpole!

BY MYSELF books are specially selected to be suitable for beginner readers. Other BY MYSELF books available from Young Corgi Books include:

MY GANG by Catherine Sefton
THE HAUNTING OF HEMLOCK HALL by Lance Salway
MIDNIGHT PIRATE by Diana Hendry
T.R. BEAR Series by Terrance Dicks
  ENTER T.R.
  T.R. GOES TO SCHOOL
  T.R.'S DAY OUT

The Killer Tadpole

Jacqueline Wilson
Illustrated by Lesley Smith

THE KILLER TADPOLE

A YOUNG CORGI BOOK 0 552 52414 X

Originally published in Great Britain in 1984 by Hamish Hamilton Children's Books.

PRINTING HISTORY

Young Corgi edition published 1987

This book is set in 14/18 pt Century Schoolbook by Colset Private Limited, Singapore.

Young Corgi Books are published by Transworld Publishers Ltd., 61 - 63 Uxbridge Road, Ealing, London W5 5SA, in Australia by Transworld Publishers (Australia) Pty. Ltd., 15 - 23 Helles Avenue, Moorebank, NSW 2170, and in New Zealand by Transworld Publishers (N.Z.) Ltd., Cnr. Moselle and Waipareira Avenues, Henderson, Auckland.

Made and printed in Great Britain by
The Guernsey Press Co. Ltd., Guernsey, Channel Islands.

The Killer Tadpole

Chapter One

'Do you want to be in my gang?' Spike hissed.

His real name was Simon, but everyone called him Spike. Spike made sure of that. He was very good at bashing people up. He was very big for his age, the biggest boy in the whole of the Infants. He always wore great big boots, even in summer. He was very good at kicking people too.

He had kicked Nicholas lots of times. He had once bashed him up properly too, punching Nicholas in the tummy. Nicholas had doubled up and cried and Spike and his gang had laughed and jeered.

So what was Spike doing, asking Nicholas if he wanted to be in his gang?

Nicholas blinked nervously at Spike. He peered quickly over his shoulder, wondering if Spike could be talking to someone else. But no, they were the only two boys in the cloakroom.

'What's the matter?' Spike demanded. 'Are you deaf or are you stupid?'

'I'm not either,' said Nicholas. He watched Spike's hard fists anxiously.

Spike took a step forward in his big

brown boots. Nicholas took a step backwards.

'So do you or don't you?' said Spike.

'Do I or don't I what?' Nicholas said, taking another step backwards.

He still had a bruise on his shins from the last time Spike had kicked him.

'Do you want to be in my gang?'

Nicholas nodded. He was too scared to do anything else.

'Then meet us after school. Down by the pond,' said Spike, and he winked as he swaggered off.

Nicholas did his best to wink back. He stood alone in the cloakroom, feeling dizzy. Spike had asked him to be in his gang! Spike only asked the really tough boys to be in his gang. Nicholas thought about it carefully. He was still scared, but he couldn't help being flattered. He puffed out his chest and practised swaggering around the cloakroom as if he was wearing big brown boots.

'You'll never guess what,' Nicholas whispered to his friend Brainbox back in the classroom.

His real name was David, but everyone called him Brainbox. Nicholas didn't know whether Brainbox minded or not. They were friends because they sat together and went home together, but Brainbox could be a bit odd at times. It was probably because he was so brainy. But even Brainbox couldn't outwit Spike and his gang. Brainbox had been bashed up lots and lots of times.

'Has Spike asked you to be in his gang?' Brainbox whispered back.

Nicholas stared at him. It was incredible the way Brainbox could always work things out.

'You ought to write those star things you get in the newspapers. Things that predict the future. I forget the name,' Nicholas whispered.

'Horoscopes,' said Brainbox. 'No fear. I'd sooner write Horror Comics.

Stories about a giant slimy snorty slobbery slug called Spike. So are you going to?'

'Am I going to what?' asked Nicholas, who was still in rather a daze.

'Are you going to be in Spike's gang?'

'Well. I don't know. I mean, I sort of said I'd meet up with him after school, but I didn't actually say . . . '

Brainbox sighed. 'If you start bashing me up too, will you let me take my glasses off first?'

'I won't ever bash you up, Brainbox. You're my friend,' said Nicholas.

'You might. If Spike told you to,' said Brainbox.

'Nicholas and David! Do stop talking and get on with your work,' called Miss Rayner, their teacher.

Nicholas risked another telling off from Miss Rayner and peered round at Spike at the back of the class. Spike gave him another wink. Nicholas fidgeted uncomfortably. He wished Spike hadn't asked him to be in his gang.

Chapter Two

'I think I'll walk home with you, Brainbox,' said Nicholas after school.

But Spike and his gang were waiting at the end of the road. Spike and Rusty and Big Angus and Jeff and Karate-Chop.

Nicholas started walking very slowly indeed. Brainbox put his glasses in his blazer pocket. But for

once the gang wasn't concerned with Brainbox.

'Hey you. Nicholas. You coming with us?' Spike called.

You didn't argue with Spike. Especially when he was with Rusty and Big Angus and Jeff and Karate-Chop.

'See you, Brainbox,' said Nicholas, his voice squeaky.

'Come on over to the pond. That's our territory, see,' said Spike. 'We've got a camp there.'

'Smashing,' said Nicholas politely. 'Only I can't stay too long, Spike, because my Mum worries if I'm late home.'

Nicholas knew it was a mistake to mention his Mum as soon as he said it.

He felt his face reddening.

'Oh dear, does his Mumsie worry then?' said Rusty.

'Does she fuss about her little Nicky then?' said Big Angus.

'Perhaps she thinks her precious little Nicky's going to wet his knickers,' said Jeff giggling.

'We don't want old Knickers in our gang, do we, Spike?' said Karate-Chop, his hands whistling through the air, very nearly hitting Nicholas.

Nicholas stood still, trying not to tremble. He was sure he was about to be bashed up.

'Pipe down, you lot,' said Spike. 'I still think he could be useful. You come with us, Knickers. We'll see how he copes with the Ordeal.'

Nicholas didn't know what an Ordeal was. He didn't like the sound of it at all. He knew his Mum really

would worry if he was late. But he went with Spike and the others to the pond.

Spike had made an impressive camp out of an old tent. He had a lot of weapons (assorted toy guns and some big sticks). He had his own personal sweet store (chocolate bars pinched from the baby class at Playtime). He even had a vehicle (a car made out of a box and some pram wheels).

Nicholas looked round the camp admiringly. Spike sat down on the biggest box. Rusty and Big Angus and Jeff and Karate-Chop sat down on boxes too. Nicholas couldn't see another box so he squatted on the ground, although it was very muddy

because they were so near the water. He could feel the mud on the seat of his trousers, soft and wet. He knew his Mum would make a fuss, but he wasn't going to mention his Mum ever again.

'So you want to be in my gang, do you, Knickers?' said Spike.

Nicholas nodded. He wondered whether to object to his horrible new name, but didn't quite dare.

'You have to be really tough to be in my gang,' said Spike. 'You have to go through Three Terrible Ordeals. Okay?'

Three!

The first ordeal was truly terrible. He had to stand without flinching while they all spat at him.

The second ordeal was even worse. He had to walk along a plank right over the pond. The pond was deep in places and Nicholas wasn't that good a swimmer. And then when he got right to the end Karate-Chop started wobbling the plank up and down deliberately. Nicholas very nearly fell in, but somehow or other he made it back to dry land.

But the third and last ordeal was

impossible. Spike collected a jam-jar full of frogspawn from the pond. He held it under Nicholas's nose.

'Bring the spoon,' said Spike, grinning.

Nicholas stared at him in horror. Rusty sniggered and produced a filthy teaspoon and dug it into the lump of frogspawn.

'You've got to swallow a spoonful,' said Spike. 'Then you can be in my gang.'

Chapter Three

Nicholas's Mum had often complained that he was a faddy eater. He had never been able to eat anything soft and slimy, like boiled eggs or yoghurt or the jelly on tinned ham.

He stared at the gleaming grey mass of frogspawn speckled with little black dots. He imagined it spooned into his mouth, sliding down the back of his throat . . .

'I can't!' he wailed, and burst into tears.

Spike and Rusty and Big Angus and Jeff and Karate-Chop laughed at him. Then they threw the frogspawn at him. Quite a lot went down his neck. Then they bashed him up. Then they turned him out of the camp.

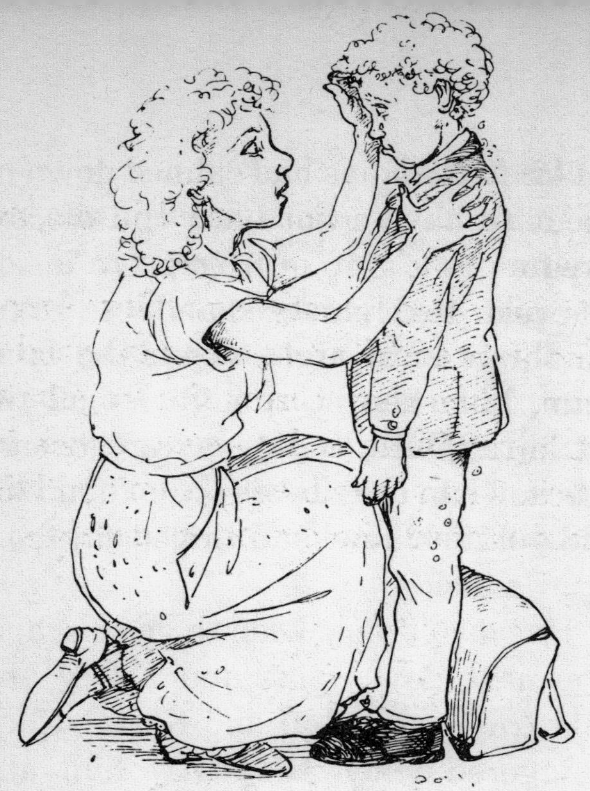

It took Nicholas a long and weary time to get home. His Mum was very cross and she got even crosser when she saw the state of his clothes. But when Nicholas started crying again Mum sat him on her lap and gave him a cuddle, even though she got mud all over her dress.

When Nicholas had calmed down he went to have a hot bath and discovered a great glob of frogspawn inside his vest. He shuddered and was going to throw it straight down the lavatory, but then he thought of all the little tadpoles leading a very dreary life down in the sewers so he found his old goldfish bowl and tipped the frogspawn inside.

He wasn't very keen to go to school the next day. Spike and Rusty and Big Angus and Jeff and Karate-Chop sniggered when they saw him and then they all pretended to cry, making silly boo-hoo-hoo noises. They called him Knickers and some of the other boys in the class started calling him Knickers too.

But not Brainbox.

They both got bashed up on the way home from school. They both

cried a bit afterwards, but it didn't matter in front of each other. Then Nicholas invited Brainbox home to tea.

Nicholas's Mum gave them baked beans on toast and salt and vinegar crisps and chocolate wafer biscuits and apples and raspberry milk shakes. Then Nicholas showed Brainbox all his favourite toys and his pet hamsters.

'This is Hammy and this is Eggy and these are their babies, Bacon and Sausage and Fried Bread,' said Nicholas. 'I'm busy training them to do special tricks. Hammy can very nearly walk on his hind legs, you know. I'm going to be an animal trainer when I grow up. I'd like to have my own circus.' Nicholas looked at the goldfish bowl. 'Maybe I could train some of the tadpoles too. When

they get to be frogs. Or do you think that's a daft idea, Brainbox?'

'You can have Performing Fleas, so I don't see why you can't have Performing Frogs,' said Brainbox.

Nicholas beamed at him.

'Even if I had been in Spike's gang I really wouldn't ever had bashed you up, Brainbox,' he said. The next morning Nicholas peered eagerly at his frogspawn. There was one black, wriggling speck which looked hopeful. He sprinkled it with stale goldfish food. Nothing much seemed to happen.

'I think they must have died of shock when they went inside my vest,' said Nicholas sadly.

'Give them another day or two,' Brainbox advised.

Brainbox was right. The next morning Nicholas saw the minute black creature swimming bravely round and round the goldfish bowl.

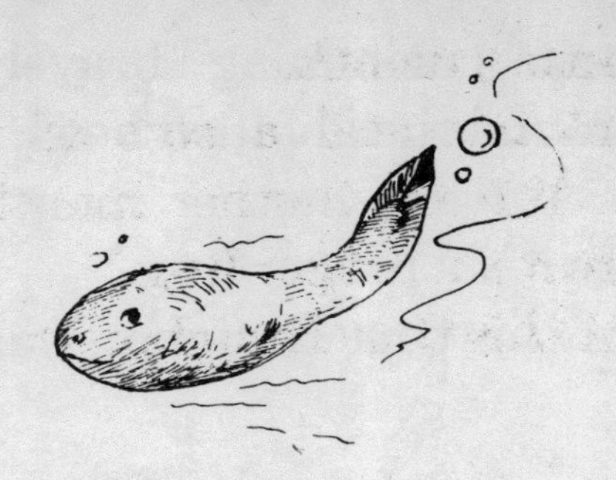

'Hello, little tadpole,' Nicholas whispered delightedly. He waggled his finger at it in a friendly greeting. 'Tell your brothers and sisters to get a move on too, will you?'

But the tadpole turned out to be an only child. None of the others developed.

'Never mind. I've still got you,' said Nicholas to the tadpole. 'Hurry up and turn into a frog and then I'll teach you to do tricks.'

Brainbox obligingly looked up tadpoles in his encyclopedia and said that it should start growing little frog legs in about a month.

'But it's still a sort of frog-pole then. It'll be another month or two before it's a proper frog.'

But this time Brainbox was wrong.

Chapter Four

The tadpole grew and grew. But it didn't grow little frog legs. It didn't grow little frog arms. It didn't lose its tail and become a proper fully grown frog. It just went on growing into a larger and larger tadpole.

'If you ask me, it's a very backward tadpole,' said Brainbox.

'If you ask me, I think it's very forward,' said Nicholas. 'It's highly intelligent, Brainbox, honest. I just have to put my hand over the bowl and it comes to the top of the water with its mouth opening and shutting before I've even sprinkled on its fishfood.'

'That's the trouble, you're giving it far too much food,' said Brainbox. 'You're just making it into the fattest tadpole in the world.'

'Hey, do you really think so? Then perhaps it could be in my circus. I could train it, couldn't I?'

The tadpole went on growing and growing. Nicholas had to buy a new packet of fishfood.

‘I thought your goldfish died, son?’ said the pet shop man.

‘I’ve got a tadpole instead,’ said Nicholas, and went red when the pet shop man roared with laughter.

‘He’ll laugh the other side of his face when you’re the chief attraction in my circus,’ he whispered to the tadpole.

DOG

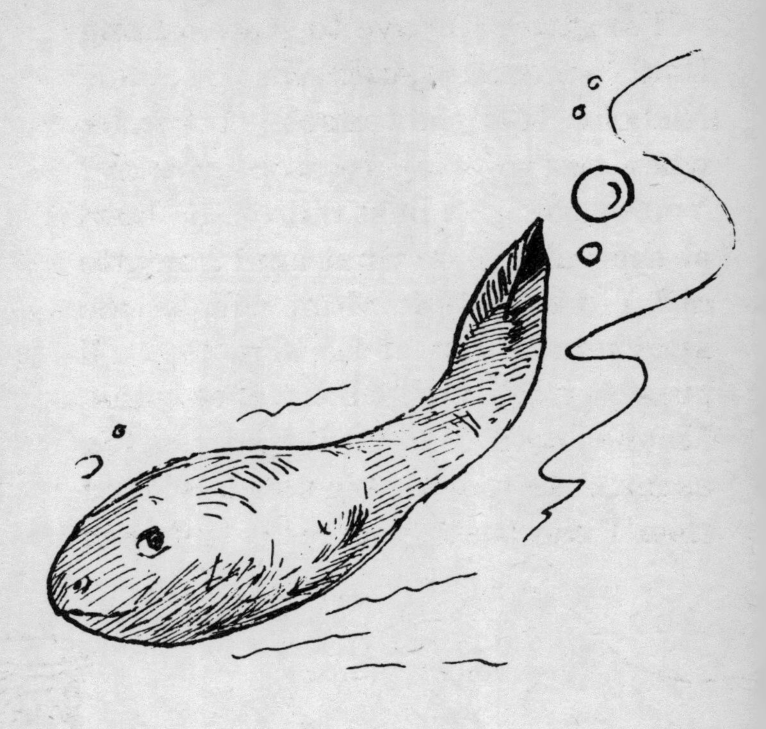

The tadpole went on growing. Nicholas started feeding it little shreds of lettuce and cabbage as a change from the fishfood, because Brainbox said that tadpoles were vegetarian.

'I'm going to have to start raiding Dad's vegetable garden for you soon,' Nicholas told the tadpole. 'I wonder when you're going to stop growing? You're going to bust out of the bowl at this rate. Then what am I going to do? I don't think Mum will let me keep you in the bath. Maybe you'll grow so huge you'll need a great tank. Maybe you'll grow until you're as big as me. A tadpole as big as a boy! And then I can teach you really amazing

tricks. You'll be better than a dolphin. And what if you *still* go on growing? What if you grow to be as big as . . . as big as . . . as big as a Killer Whale? Wow! We could have our own special

show. I could get in the tank with you and ride on your back. The Killer Tadpole!'

Nicholas was so excited that he couldn't keep quiet. He talked about his tadpole to everyone. Mum and Dad nodded and went 'Mmm' and 'Really' and 'Yes, Nick', but he could tell they weren't really listening. Nicholas talked about his tadpole to Brainbox instead. He talked about his tadpole so long and so loudly that everyone else heard too. Even Spike.

'What you going on about, Knickers? Have you gone loopy? What do

you mean, a Killer Tadpole?' said Spike.

Spike sniggered. Rusty and Big Angus and Jeff and Karate-Chop sniggered too. Brainbox put his hand to his glasses nervously. But Nicholas stood his ground and stuck his chin out.

'It's true,' he said. 'I've got the biggest tadpole in the whole world. And it's getting bigger every day. If

you don't believe me, come round to my house and I'll show you.'

'Okay,' said Spike. 'Me and my gang will be round after school.'

'Do I have to come too?' Brainbox whispered.

Nicholas's Mum wasn't too pleased when Nicholas and Brainbox and Spike and Rusty and Big Angus and Jeff and Karate-Chop came home to tea. She gave them all baked beans on toast but they had to share three chocolate biscuits between them.

Then they all went up to Nicholas's room to see the Killer Tadpole. It didn't look quite Killer standard yet.

'That's not a tadpole!' Spike yelled. 'That's a *fish*, a silly little tiddler out the pond.'

Spike and Rusty and Big Angus and Jeff and Karate-Chop howled with laughter. They didn't bash

Yum Yum
CHOC BAR

Nicholas and Brainbox because they were still too full of baked beans, but they said a lot of insulting things.

It didn't look as big as usual. Not very big at all. But it was still undeniably the biggest tadpole in the whole world.

When they went home at last Nicholas and Brainbox looked at the Killer Tadpole for a long time.

'I think it might be a fish,' Nicholas said eventually.

'We are thick,' said Brainbox. 'And they call me Brainbox.'

'I don't like nicknames. I'm going to call you David from now on,' said Nicholas. 'David, I've been thinking. Shall we have our own gang? Just a little one. We won't let anyone else join. Especially not Spike and his lot. And David – have you ever heard of a Performing Tiddler?'

MY GANG

BY CATHERINE SEFTON
ILLUSTRATED BY CATHERINE BRADBURY

'This is my gang, Noel!' said Marty. 'It's girls only, and we're tough. We'll wallop you if you start mucking things up! Right, gang?'

Being looked after by his big sister and her gang is no joke for Noel, especially as they won't let him join. But soon Noel finds a way of making sure that he is not the only one left out . . .

0 552 524158 £1.50

MIDNIGHT PIRATE

BY DIANA HENDRY
ILLUSTRATED BY JANET DUCHESNE

'Oh Pirate, dear little Pirate,' whispered Ida, 'you can't stay here. The Aunts don't want a kitten.'

Nothing Ida could say would make the Aunts change their minds and it seemed as though the tiny kitten she had found under the holly bush would have to stay out in the cold and wet, unloved by anyone.

But the kitten had other ideas and even the Aunts became involved in what happened next . . .

0 552 524174 £1.50

THE HAUNTING OF HEMLOCK HALL

BY LANCE SALWAY
ILLUSTRATED BY CATHIE SHUTTLEWORTH

'There's no ghosts at Hemlock Hall. Never have been and never will,' the old gardener tells Tom when he comes to work there in the holidays.

But the awful new owners, the Trotters, have other ideas. When they open the Hall to the public, they are determined that ghosts shall be among its many attractions . . .

0 552 524166 £1.50

A DRAGON IN CLASS 4

BY JUNE COUNSEL

One morning on his way to school Sam rescues a young dragon trapped in the chains of a swing. Scales – as the dragon is called – decides to join Class 4 and he brings lots of fun to Sam and his friends.

Scales becomes Sam's special friend and he helps him with his spelling and in fighting off the school bully.

'Don't worry, I'll look after you,' says the dragon. 'I've always wanted a boy of my own!'

An amusing and lively fantasy for young readers.

0 552 523135 £1.50

A BIT OF GIVE AND TAKE

BY BERNARD ASHLEY

'A kitten? You don't reckon you're keeping that, do you?' said Scott's Mum.

'I am. I saved it from death,' Scott shouted, 'He'll die without me!'

When Scott saves a kitten trapped in a rubbish bin, he takes it home despite the council rule about no pets. Scott is determined to keep Scrap, as he names the kitten, although it gets him into a lot of trouble . . .

0 552 523488 £1.50

If you would like to receive a Newsletter about our new Children's books, just fill in the coupon below with your name and address (or copy it onto a separate piece of paper if you don't want to spoil your book) and send it to:

The Children's Books Editor
Young Corgi Books
61–63 Uxbridge Road,
Ealing
London W5 5SA

Please send me a Children's Newsletter:

Name . . . .

Address . . . .

. . . .

. . . .

All the books on the previous pages are available at your local bookshop or can be ordered direct from the publishers: Cash Sales Dept., Transworld Publishers Ltd., 61–63 Uxbridge Road, Ealing, London W5 5SA.

Please enclose the cost of the book(s), together with the following for postage and packing costs:

Orders up to a value of £5.00	50p
Orders of a value over £5.00	Free

Please note that payment should be made by cheque or postal order in £ sterling.